Two
Tiny
Mice
Explore

For Raymond

A Templar Book

First published in the UK in 2006 by Templar Publishing,
an imprint of The Templar Company plc,
Pippbrook Mill, London Road,
Dorking, Surrey, RH4 IJE, UK
www.templarco.co.uk

Copyright © 2006 by Alan Baker

First edition

All rights reserved

ISBN-13: 978-I-840II-198-9
ISBN-10: I-840II-198-4

Edited by Ruth Martin

Printed in Hong Kong

Alan Baker's

Two Tiny Mice *Explore*

A Natural World Adventure

templar publishing

"Let's search for the riverside, it's such a lovely day."

The **harvest mice** begin their quest but do not know the way.

First they cross a
meadow where
a handsome
pheasant strides.

"We're off on an
adventure, to find
the riverside."

"Can I come along with you?"
squeaks lively little shrew.

Says playful **vole**, up on a branch,
"I wish I could come, too!"

They see a perky **pine marten** who's stopped to stand and stare

at a busy, buzzy bumblebee hovering in the air.

They ask the farmyard **ram** to tell them if he knows the way.

"Go and ask the dormouse, who lives amongst the hay."

Climbing carefully up a twig, the daring **dormouse** cries, "I spy the riverside ahead, right before my eyes!"

"At last, we've reached
the riverside!"
the harvest mice
both cry.

And as they watch
two graceful **swans**
go gliding slowly by.

Clambering through
the ivy leaves
comes **toad**,
all fat and green.

He asks about
their journey
to find out
who they've seen.

Up above a **kingfisher** is fluttering in the sky,
and sprightly **swallow** shows the mice…

how swiftly he can fly.

Then they glimpse
the farmer's **cat,**
so keep well
out of sight.

The sky is
turning inky-blue,
as daylight turns
to night.

When darkness falls
the mice can see
the silent **tawny owl**,

as night-time creatures
now creep out
to start their
midnight prowl.

Our harvest mice now scurry home
and climb into their nest.
All safe inside, 'til morning comes,
they snuggle up and rest.

Tomorrow their adventures
could take them far and wide,
as they explore the beauty
of the open countryside.

Nature Notes

The Harvest Mouse

The harvest mouse can be found among crops, long grasses or reed beds. Its long tail grips tall stems allowing it to move easily from stalk to stalk.

To keep its babies safe from predators, the harvest mouse builds a woven nest of grasses high up in the tallest stems.

Climbing among the grasses, the harvest mouse finds seeds, fruit or bulbs to eat.

A harvest mouse will also eat roots and fungi, and occasionally insects.

As winter approaches, the mouse stores away food supplies underground. Then, when food is in short supply, it spends most of its time underground, until new seeds and fruit appear in warmer weather.

Dusk is the best time to spot a harvest mouse, although they are active both night and day.

The Pheasant

Male pheasants are plump with golden-brown and black markings, a dark greenish-blue head and a red face. The females are much more dull, pale brown in colour, but both have long tail feathers.

Found mainly in parks and woodland, these large birds forage on the ground for grain, seeds, berries, roots and shoots.

The female pheasant lays eggs in a simple hollow in the ground. Her chicks are able to fly just two weeks after hatching. The mother and chicks then roost in the tree-tops out of danger from predators such as foxes.

The Shrew

During the day and night, the water shrew is busy finding worms, snails, fish, spiders and frogs to eat. It burns energy very quickly, so it must eat frequently.

Found mainly near rivers, lakes, ponds and marshes, the water shrew has glossy dark fur on its back and a white underside.

It paddles fast in water and must come to shore frequently to rest and dry its fur. Each shrew has a burrow in the bank, sometimes with an underwater entrance. It has sharp teeth and may even have poisonous saliva to prevent prey from struggling free as the shrew carries it to shore.

The Water Vole

Burrowing into the banks of slow-moving rivers and streams, the water vole builds a grass-lined nest. It prefers riverside areas with tall grasses that provide cover and food. Steep, soft, treeless banks are best for burrowing.

Coming out both during the day and at night, it feeds on grasses and other plants along the water's edge.

The water vole has thick fur, dark eyes and small hairy ears. With its round face and hairy tail, it is a true member of the vole family, though it is commonly known as the water rat.

The Pine Marten

Balancing in high branches using its bushy tail, the pine marten can climb up trees just like a cat or a squirrel.

It builds a nest inside a tree trunk, or takes over an empty squirrel's nest. Up to five babies are born in a litter each spring and cared for by their mother.

At night, the playful pine marten comes down from the trees to find mice, insects, squirrels, fruit, berries and beetles to eat. Up in the branches, the pine marten also finds birds and their eggs to eat.

The Ram

A ram is a male sheep, and the female is called a ewe. Sheep live in groups called flocks and follow the other members everywhere they go. This offers the sheep protection from predators and ensures that they all find food together.

For centuries, sheep have been farmed for their wool and their meat. While most are kept on farms, some do still live in the wild. Sheep feed mainly on grass, but farmers also give them hay and grain.

Lambs are born in spring or summer, when the weather is warmer and the grass is growing.

The Dormouse

Little dormice spend up to three quarters of their lives asleep in round nests made from grass, moss, leaves and bark. Sleeping helps to save energy, so that they can survive even when food supplies are low.

The common dormouse has a thick, bushy tail, brownish-orange fur and a pale underside.

Found in woodland and hedgerows, it can climb up as far as the tops of trees to find acorns, nuts, seeds, fruit and insects to eat.

The Swan

Elegant and graceful, the large, white mute swan is the most common wild swan in Britain. It can be found on lakes, canals and slow-moving rivers.

Plunging its long neck under the water, the swan finds water plants to eat, as well as some small water insects and occasionally small fish.

Swans live in pairs for life. They build nests on the ground from twigs, ready to hold up to nine large eggs. Baby swans, called cygnets, start life with fluffy grey feathers called down. If the nest is threatened, a male swan can be quite aggressive.

The Toad

Most toads can be told apart from frogs by their dry, warty skin, fat bodies and short hind legs.

They live on land but find lakes, ponds and rivers during the breeding season.

Feeding on worms, insects, spiders, slugs, and even mice and small snakes, toads use their long, sticky tongues to grab passing prey.

A toad lives alone and comes out of its burrow at night to forage. It does not hop like a frog, but walks instead. An irritating substance on its skin gives the toad a very unpleasant taste that keeps it safe from most predators.

The Kingfisher

Bright-coloured feathers in shades of bluish-green, orange and white make the kingfisher a very striking little bird.

Watching for insects and fish, the kingfisher is found by rivers, lakes and ponds, perching high in the trees waiting to dive into the water after its prey.

In spring, the female kingfisher lays up to ten eggs in a burrow in the riverbank. Both male and female kingfishers guard the eggs until they hatch and then feed the baby birds with young fish.

The Swallow

With skilful flight, the swallow catches insects in the air by swooping and soaring.

Recognisable by its forked tail, dark blue, shiny feathers and red face, the swallow is seen in Britain during the summer months before it migrates to Africa in the winter.

Nests of mud, grass and feathers are built high on ledges in farm outbuildings. Up to six baby swallows hatch out from their eggs and are fed by both parents.

The noisy swallow uses various calls to communicate and warns others of danger with a loud, sharp cry.

The Cat

Domestic cats are among the most popular pets in the world. As well as being affectionate companions, cats are good hunters and are often kept on farms to keep the populations of rats and mice under control.

With sharp eyesight, strong hearing and sensitive whiskers, the cat hunts best at night. Its long tail gives the cat excellent balance, so it can climb trees with ease and always land safely.

Cats can be many colours: tabby, tortoiseshell, ginger, black, white or grey, but they all have sharp claws and strong teeth to help them catch their prey.

The Tawny Owl

Swooping at speed with sharp claws, the tawny owl is an impressive hunter. At night this owl surveys its territory with large black eyes, hunting birds, frogs, insects and small mammals.

The spooky 'twit-twoo' call of the tawny owl is actually the two separate calls of the male and female communicating.

A male and female owl will live together for life, producing eggs early each spring. When the eggs hatch, the male supplies the whole family with food at first. The female only begins to hunt again after about ten days, still keeping an eye on the nest.